I0737173

An Atavic Fear of Hailstorms

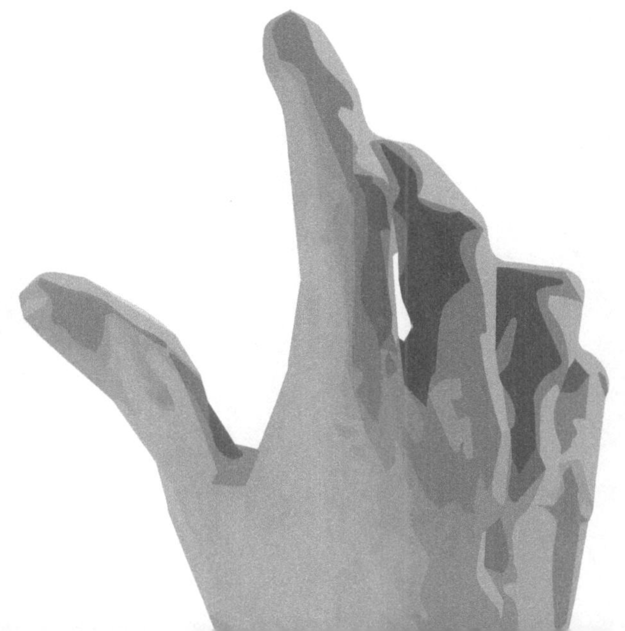

An Atavic Fear of Hailstorms

João Reis

Long Day Press
Chicago // New York

Copyright © 2023 João Reis
Published by Long Day Press
Chicago, Il 60647
LongDayPress.com
@LongDayPress

ISBN 9781950987290

Library of Congress Control Number: 2023932321

Edited by Joseph Demes
Layout by Joshua Bohnsack

Printed in the United States of America
First Edition

PROUD MEMBER

[clmp]

He had fallen asleep and crashed his car on the motorway. I suddenly fell asleep. I can't remember falling asleep, so it must have been all of a sudden, he told his friend in the hospital. Of course, we always fall asleep suddenly, for we are awake one moment and the next we aren't, and it happened the same way with me, he said in a deep philosophical bout while touching his legs and dragging his fingers over the skin up to his crotch, to make sure once again that he was missing nothing, nothing at all. But sometimes we feel we're close to falling asleep before actually falling asleep, even though we can't but not to fall asleep, he said, and he too had felt himself on the verge of falling asleep on previous occasions when driving, he had felt sleepy when driving several times indeed, yet not when he had had his latest and, so far, most serious car accident. He hadn't felt sleepy at all before falling asleep, nevertheless he had fallen asleep and hit a guardrail. His car was a wreck, it was beyond repair, a mesh of metallic sheets, glass and wires, and it should be in the scrap yard by then, but he wasn't sure, he had no way of knowing if his car was in a scrap yard or still being towed on its way to a scrap yard, and if it was in a scrap yard, it might still be exactly as it had been after the accident, or else already being scrapped piece by piece, he confided to his friend the visitor. He'd rather find out it was already being scrapped, so he could get some money out of it as soon as possible, but he doubted his car was being scrapped as of now, since he had suffered the accident only three days before, and the insurance company was probably investigating the matter, which made it quite impossible to scrap the car, yes, no one would scrap his car before some inspector from the insurance company took a look at it. On the other hand, three days was a long time to impound a crashed car. On one hand, three days was a short time for the car to get scrapped, and, on the other hand, it was a long time for it to be impounded. Hence, he assumed his car had been towed to a scrap yard but had yet to be scrapped. He was a logic-driven person, after all.

He was sitting on his bed, his friend on a chair facing him. Are you comfortable on there?, he asked his friend. Because that chair doesn't look comfortable at all, he said to his friend. I've never used it, but it looks quite rough, he added, though I've never used it, to be sure, he said, then pointing with both hands to his casted legs. He had been lying or sitting on his bed ever since he had been admitted to the hospital, with the exception of a few hours he had spent in an operating room. In short, he had never had any opportunity to sit in that seemingly uncomfortable chair. His friend replied that he didn't find the chair uncomfortable, though he had barely spent ten minutes there. He hadn't even spent ten minutes in his friend's room, so he hadn't spent ten minutes on that chair. Perhaps later his friend would find it uncomfortable.

He the patient then proceeded to tell his friend the visitor about the surgery, which he hadn't witnessed, of course, but whose effects he had been feeling since waking up from anaesthesia. First, he had felt groggy and confused, then dizzy, and at last he had vomited. He had vomited all over his bed and over the nurse who had come to his aid. The nurse had dismissed the situation as completely normal… it's normal… absolutely normal!… though he hadn't been capable of hiding his disgust for having so much vomit, and such a yellowish-orange vomit at that, all over his arms and chest. That nurse had tattooed arms, and his tattooed arms were covered in vomit, for he the patient couldn't stop retching and vomiting after waking up from anaesthesia. The nurse even called a doctor, though he had begun by telling him it was all normal, as many patients vomited after waking up from anaesthesia, and some of them would vomit for hours. A few would vomit for two or three days in a row, which was a bit concerning. Thus having vomited for only half an hour after waking up from anaesthesia, he shouldn't worry himself much over it. Anyways, the nurse had rung a bell and called a doctor though the intercom the second time he had got covered in vomit, and a yellowish-orange vomit at that. I hadn't eaten anything the evening before to avoid vomiting and suffocating in vomit while they operated on my legs, he told his friend. Nevertheless, he had vomited after waking up from anaesthesia, he hadn't eaten any dinner the evening before, he had only drunk liquids, but he had somehow thrown up a yellowish-orange vomit. Don't you worry, that happened yesterday, today I haven't vomited at all, he assured his friend. His friend could feel at ease, as he didn't intend to vomit that afternoon or that evening and not even that night, he the visitor could relax and talk to his friend the patient, but he didn't relax, he was uneasy and increasingly so, each minute he felt more and more uneasy, and he began wondering if he should go home, in fact he asked himself why he was there, maybe he shouldn't have visited his friend, he'd probably be home in a few days, back home with two broken casted legs, he could have visited him later, after all, they weren't that close friends, he had only known about the accident through another common acquaintance, and he the visitor could have brought him the patient a couple of beers or something to snack on if he had visited him at his house, namely the patient's home, but instead he had taken only a postcard to his friend the patient, because he couldn't bring beers to the hospital, and he actually didn't know if his friend liked drinking beer, proof that they weren't such close friends after all. One assumes two close friends would know if the other enjoyed drinking beer, but he didn't know if his injured friend enjoyed beer, or whether drank beer at all or just drank beer when meeting his friends, thus being a so-called *social drinker*, perhaps he didn't appreciate the taste of beer or the smell of beer or both the taste and the smell of beer but he drank some beer anyway just to be socially accepted. Now his friend the visitor didn't enjoy beer that much, at least pilsner, he did enjoy some stouts, honestly, he wasn't particularly fond of the taste and smell of any beer whatsoever, he drank beer mostly for social reasons, to enjoy his friends' company, to mingle with them, to be part of the posse, they all laughed while drinking beer, his friends perhaps did not enjoy beer that much and only pretended to enjoy it in order to be accepted, them too, as part of the group, he himself was a so-called social drinker, despite all his efforts to look and sound like a real beer connoisseur, he would often praise the beers he was tasting or drinking, pretending to ingest them with gusto, *when in truth he could barely stand the smell and the taste of most beers*, a few he enjoyed tasting and smelling, most of them he didn't enjoy at all, and when drinking some pilsners he *even had to refrain from spitting them out* and sometimes *he had to contain a proto-retching urge* quickly deriving from stomach sickness, so he couldn't be sure if his injured friend was a so-called social beer drinker or a real enthusiast of beer, there was no way of knowing it unless he paid attention to his injured friend once he saw him drinking beer again, nevertheless, whether he the patient enjoyed drinking beer or not was a secondary question, for the main question was whether he did drank beer at all, because he had tried to recall his friend drinking beer and he couldn't remember seeing him drinking beer, for as much as he tried he couldn't recollect a single occasion in which he had seen his friend the patient drinking beer or even touching a bottle or jug or glass of beer, which proved they weren't such good friends and that he could have avoided this visit altogether.

A nurse entered the room, he looked at the visitor, said good afternoon and asked if everything was ok, the patient replied, he said everything was ok, he didn't need anything, then the nurse turned his back on them and went away closing the door behind him. The nurse was a young man, and his friend the visitor asked the patient if that nurse was the nurse he had vomited on, and he the patient nodded, yes, it was him I threw up on, all right, he said to his friend, and presently asked him the visitor if could find the TV remote control anywhere, for he didn't have it with him and now it was too late to call back the nurse and ask him for the remote control, or not too late but decidedly much more embarrassing, he could indeed call the nurse back to his room but he didn't feel like it, for it would be embarrassing to call him and ask for the TV remote control. It would be embarrassing in any situation, to call a medical professional and ask him for a remote control always seemed embarrassing, to him at least, quite embarrassing, as it could be seen as a proof of disrespect, he couldn't simply ring the bell and ask the nurse for the remote control, so this was embarrassing in any possible situation, and even more in that particular situation, it would be most embarrassing to call the nurse back into the room for the sake of a lost TV remote control when moments before that same nurse had just asked the patient if everything was ok and whether or not he needed anything. Perhaps it wouldn't be so embarrassing if he rang the bell and another nurse showed up in his room, maybe it would be less embarrassing than having the same nurse coming back into his room, however, it would still be somewhat embarrassing to call a nurse to get him to fetch a TV remote control, and if he rang the bell right now he would probably get the same nurse coming into his room once again, and then asking him for the TV remote control would be extremely embarrassing, so he the patient pondered this matter in detail but didn't say anything to his friend the visitor, who was turning around in his chair looking for the remote control before finally getting up to search for it all over the room.

He the visitor found the remote control at last, he gave it to his friend the invalid on the bed, who turned the TV on and gave the remote control back to his friend the visitor. He the patient looked at the screen lighting up, asked his friend to sit down again, please sit down, he said, did you watch the match last evening?, he then added just for the sake of keeping some conversation going, for he the patient didn't even know if his friend the visitor enjoyed football and watching football, if he enjoyed watching football matches, whether live on TV or in the stadium, he didn't know that nor if he was a fan of any of the two teams that had played the match the previous evening, though he might not be a fan of any of the two teams and still have watched the match just for pleasure, out of a football lover's joy in watching a match, only for the sake of sports, out of a pure pleasure for football, so he didn't know if his friend would actually want to watch the game, proof again they weren't close friends, and in fact he had been baffled when he had seen him entering the room, he wasn't expecting many visits, and he wasn't at all expecting his visit, because they barely knew each other, and he might have thought what *that stupid son of a bitch* was doing there. In the beginning, upon his friend's arrival, he even had to try and remember his friend's name, so it's highly probable that he did indeed think what *that stupid son of a bitch* was doing there. He knew his name of course, though it was a bit fuzzy, a name among several possible names, he then hit on it, his friend's name, and he asked his friend how he was doing while feeling quite flabbergasted at his presence, he wasn't expecting him at that moment or at any moment whatsoever, in fact he wasn't expecting anyone at that exact moment, perhaps he hoped to get more visits, although not from that particular friend, but later, not so early in the afternoon, so he was indeed scratching himself above the cast on both legs, he was scratching himself when his friend arrived. He himself wasn't fond of football or most sports, as a kid he enjoyed watching a match with his dad or grandpa, but not anymore, he would decline his father's invitations to watch matches on TV, he couldn't be bothered with that anymore, he had been reflecting during the match, the previous evening when he had found out a football match was being broadcasted from the noises around him, televisions turned on in adjacent rooms. He hadn't turned his TV on, rather he had been reflecting alone, thinking about her, he often travelled to meet her, she smiled when they met, she always smiled when they met, maybe he smiled too, he couldn't know, he didn't see himself reflected in a mirror or a pool of water whenever he met her, it was a tragedy!... actually, he had not seen his face reflected anywhere on any surface not even once when meeting her, hence he couldn't know if he too smiled at her once he arrived to meet her, perhaps he put on a moronic face, a natural mask of awkwardness-driven stupidity... later he would smile, of course, he couldn't help but to smile, her face her light-brown hair not that long hair bobbed-hair strong beautiful hair, it suited her so much, wasn't that marvellous?, everything about her suited her, a miracle!, hands hair neck eyes nose ears the ears of an elf chin cheeks shoulders collarbones, everything suited her, her fragile collarbone he wanted to kiss it he dreamt of kissing it of kissing and licking her collarbone and all her body her elf ears all her vertebrae from C1 to coccyx all her bones suited her, skin flesh tendons arteries, marvellous indeed, and quite salty and tasty, he would drive kilometres to see her, kilometres of tar, asphalt swallowed by his car, his foot on the gas pedal, almost the entire way with his foot on the gas pedal, rarely pressing the brake, rarely changing gear, guardrails, signal posts, bridges, tunnels, trees, gas stations, lorries, cars, motorbikes, more cars, on the day of the accident he had mostly been following another car, at that time of the day there wasn't a lot of traffic on the road, it was an important motorway but strangely enough there was not much traffic at that time on that particular day, a blue Volvo had been on his tail, then he overtook him, he followed the blue Volvo closely for a few kilometres, then he moved to the left lane to overtake both the blue Volvo and a lorry, the blue Volvo also overtook the lorry and got behind him, following his car for many kilometres, only he and the blue Volvo on long stretches of road, he overtook a couple of lorries, the blue Volvo took to the left lane and followed him while overtaking the lorries, two cars driving in the same direction, keeping each other company, he hadn't known if the Volvo's driver was a man or a woman, that was irrelevant, it was a blue Volvo, he felt like he was going back to his childhood when vehicles had a life of their own, to a time when one could meet a nice vehicle, a bad vehicle, all vehicles had the potential to be good vehicles for they hid their drivers inside them, thus creating a veil of anonymity extending from the four-wheeled vehicle drivers to the helmeted motorcyclists. As he didn't see any of their drivers, all vehicles were potentially good, and they in fact acquired good, positive human traits their owners or drivers lacked, he could look at a white Fiat and find it a nice, polite, good-mannered car, while its owner was a filthy unpolite man who belched and said you're too thin, you need to eat more, or so, any girlfriends?, and then proceed to talk about football, football again, and TV programs and food and cheap wine and to belch and scratch himself, once this greasy man got back behind the wheel his Fiat lost half or all of its personality and image, at least from a short distance, when he could be seen at the wheel, after he had met and talked to him, thus confirming the rancid character of that individual in particular, that man smeared his Fiat with his greasiness, with his head bobbing up and down above the dashboard he soiled that Fiat's spirit, the Fiat's lights lost their character, suddenly they weren't eyes anymore, he the patient couldn't see them as the eyes of a living talking thinking car, once he could see all vehicles cars motorbikes lorries loaders vans fire engines ambulances patrol cars concrete mixers all vehicles looked like friendly beings until they got soiled, but now he the patient couldn't see any vehicle as a friendly being, he could do it no more and could never ever do it again, he had lost that capacity many years ago, now he was driving and that blue Volvo was just a blue car, a

Volvo, newer and more expensive than his car, those were the details he could see now, in his childhood he would find vehicles friendly or not so friendly, some were actually not so nice, some vehicles full of mud their lights broken rust on their hoods doors they were sinister, villains on the road, now he couldn't see good or evil in cars, only their brands and how expensive they were, he wasn't a car man, a man interested in cars, but he noticed how old and how expensive the cars were, he didn't know anything about car prices, still he evaluated them on the basis of their makes and ages, that one was expensive for sure, this one is a crap. That blue Volvo was quite expensive, as all new Volvos are, it was far more expensive than his car and newer, too, nevertheless the blue Volvo followed on his tail for many kilometres, the motorway rolled over plains and hills, forests and villages, the blue Volvo followed him even when he was overtaking other vehicles, always keeping pace with him, then after an exit the blue Volvo had followed him while overtaking a lorry but hadn't resumed its position behind his the patient's car, no, he kept in the left lane after overtaking the lorry and overtook him the patient, too, then he sped ahead, he the patient followed the blue Volvo for several more kilometres, maybe seven kilometres, perhaps eight or nine, probably not ten, in the end the blue Volvo disappeared and he the patient drove alone towards his destination, he wasn't exactly alone, of course, there were other vehicles on the road, some driving in the same direction, some in the opposite direction, the blue Volvo was being driven by a man, a bald man, a bald middle-aged man who somewhat *soiled* that blue Volvo, the blue Volvo lost part of its charm when the bald man overtook his the patient's car, allowing him the patient to see that the blue Volvo driver was in fact a *bald middle-aged man*, the driver could be anything or anyone and still not soil the blue Volvo, for he the patient was an adult man now, he only took notice of the car's make and its eventual value, but that bald man had somehow smeared the blue Volvo, for although he had not envisioned its driver at all and had accepted the a priori possibility of the blue Volvo being driven by anyone on earth, in truth he the patient had not imagined the blue Volvo's driver as a bald middle-aged man at all, and moreover as *that particular bald middle-aged man*, so he had lost both his company on the motorway and his unconscious illusions.

He drove towards his destination, her city, her house, southward, there were not many cars on the road yet, one could assume there would be more cars as time passed by and he neared the city, but there weren't, he was impatient, as always he was eager to see her, to be with her, oh if only she was more flexible and could accept the truth as it was, then she'd be perfect... but she was perfect as she was, of course... completely perfect... a perfect sphere... devoid of angles in which muck could gather... no, on that sphere one couldn't find a single speck of dust... yes... she was perfect just throw that despicable thought out of the window, please, she couldn't be more flexible at all!, he concluded as he kept driving, he turned up the music, the sky was overcast, gray clouds gathering ever more, clusters of dark clouds over the motorway, he wasn't afraid of rain even when driving on a motorway, he didn't fear the water on the asphalt whenever overtaking a lorry blinding him with a sea of rain splashing against his windshield, he might fear hailstorms a bit more, sometimes hail could fall to earth as big icy rocks, though in general hail assumed the form of small ice balls, it could fall upon earth and thus motorways as big heavy ice balls, these hard balls could crush his windshield, it was unusual but still possible, it wasn't so rare as that, being hit by lighting was rarer and people still feared thunderstorms, people indeed had an atavic fear of thunderstorms, so they could most naturally have an atavic fear of hailstorms, not only farmers who had much to lose if hail hit their crops, but also drivers, both professional drivers and people in general who had to make use of the public road system during a hailstorm, he had no crops of his own despite his long time wish of having crops, or not exactly crops, rather a small or medium sized vegetable garden whence he could go to wander off and pick some fruits and vegetables, perhaps there he would be safer than on the motorway, in fact he had never had a major accident before, only a few small hits, never his fault, no, absolutely not, he had never been at fault, once he had to stop in a traffic queue at a roundabout exit and a lady hit his car from behind... from behind... he was not moving at all... after they had left their respective cars, the lady asked him how he had done that... oh, I don't know *how you did this*... she asked him how he could have done that… he was waiting for the queue to move… she was in a hurry… she couldn't stop… she had to pick her fifteen year-old son from school… he might die of exposure or undernourishment if she didn't get there on time… or maybe get lost in the streets and never get back home… she obviously tried to manoeuvre her car around his, the patient's, car… but she didn't manoeuvre the car at all… she couldn't do it… something must have happened… she miscalculated the distance… and she hit his car from behind… his car shook all over… and then the question… how could he have done that?… he didn't know… for sure he didn't know how he could have waited, completely still, in a queue and *made that lady hit him from behind*… it was a big mystery… then they had filled out the insurance papers… he was in the right, he felt safe, moved on, took care of his errands, the insurance company would pay for the damage… still the insurance company hadn't paid for the damage… the pen drawing on the insurance papers was not explicit enough… they couldn't see the cars clearly enough in the picture… and previously he had had only one accident, an old man had abruptly changed lanes, he hadn't braked in time, that time yes, the insurance company had paid for the damage, once again he had been in the right, not surprisingly!, he had had those two accidents but never before a serious accident, now he had hit a guardrail, his car was crushed, he had gotten stuck inside the wreckage, he couldn't get out, the firemen had to take him out of his car, he had two broken legs, he was complaining by the time the fire truck arrived at the spot, an ambulance and a police car had arrived soon afterwards, he had been transferred to the nearest hospital, she was waiting for him at her home, time passed by and he was in the hospital and hadn't yet talked to her, once he checked his mobile phone he noticed she had called and sent him a couple of messages, where are you? are you late?; are you ok?, the latest message had been sent more than twenty minutes ago, he tried to reply, his mobile phone was inside one of his trousers pockets, he asked a nurse to get it for him, despite the painkillers they had already given him it was too painful to take it out, the nurse helped him to take the phone out of his pocket, here you go, she said, he had to reply quickly, for he was to be cat scanned, the doctors wanted to scan his legs, he wrote a message, there's a problem, I can't be there today, he didn't tell her about the accident, later he would tell her about the accident. He wished to know how injured he was before telling her about the accident, he didn't want to tell her he had had an accident *while driving to meet her*. He sent the message, waited some moments for a reply. Please give me your phone for a minute or two, sir, we need to get you to the scan room, the nurse told him, and so he gave her his phone, by that time she hadn't answered yet. He felt a bit disgusted, the nurse was doing her job, of course, but people were prone to interrupt and annoy other people at the most inconvenient moments, he felt frustrated, irritation swelling up inside him, to be around and surrounded by people was *frustrating* and at the same time *necessary*, and indeed even more frustrating for being necessary, how could he get out of the car and get treated if it weren't for other people, someone had called the emergency number, the firemen had freed him from the wreckage, the paramedics had taken care of him during the transport to the hospital, so he too needed people, though truth be told perhaps he wouldn't need people if people hadn't built motorways and cars, in that instance he wouldn't have crashed his car against a guardrail and he wouldn't have broken his two legs at the same time, anyway he could have broken his two legs at the same time even if cars and motorways hadn't been invented at all, he might have broken one or both his legs while trying to climb a tree or running away from some danger, and then he would have one or two legs broken and be defenceless, helpless, he would die alone in the wilderness or be left behind by his tribe, if he had a tribe, his carcass would rot and be ingested by scavengers and worms, feeding the vermin he would remain alone it's true, nonetheless he would like to avoid feeding the worms for some more years yet, henceforth there were some advantages to having people close to him, surrounding him or not, maybe he could avoid closer contacts somehow, except for at the moment, as he was lying on a stretcher, he needed people to move him around, he was now being scanned, his mobile phone in a place unknown, they proceeded to scan his legs, it's ok now, breathe normally, the doctor said.

Despite knowing that he needed people whom

he could live with, societally speaking, in order to survive the harsh conditions earth imposed on its inhabitants, humans included, for the planet and nature want to kill us the sooner the better, and society keeps us alive but also kills us, just like nature, both nature and society *keep us alive and kill us at the same time*, he thought to himself while being scanned, nature and society together allow us to live but at a certain point end up injuring or killing us, he the patient thought to himself when the doctors scanned his legs, well, despite needing people, he would try to avoid them whenever possible, and by then they had removed him from the cat-scan machine. His legs would indeed need some screws and plates, he needed surgery, a potentially fatal surgery, as all surgeries are potentially fatal, so once again society was mingling with nature to keep him alive and simultaneously injuring him just to, at the last moment, kill him: they together had commingled to get him half-crushed in a wrecked car and now they were commingling to save him, nevertheless he would need weeks or months to recover from that accident, weeks and months skin-itching and feeble-legging in this world, it was a dark future, yet not so dark that he had had a spinal injury, he was glad, paramedics and doctors and nurses and people around him cheered for him for having escaped a scary spinal injury, hurrah!, they gave him thumbs up whenever they learned of how he had had a car accident and escaped a much feared spinal injury, they all cheered for him even though they knew he might be operated on, they all had congratulated him, since he was not so old that he should face those two broken legs as a life threatening occurrence, he had time and energy and health and youth enough to fully recover, he might limp afterwards, though, anyway he shouldn't die of those broken legs, unless he died *during the surgery*, of course, it was possible even though not probable, so he shouldn't die like many old people who break a leg or two, in old age breaking a leg can be fatal, whether the old person dies during the surgery, from a stroke from not moving their limbs while recovering, or simply from waiting, lying on the ground far from the phone, that a neighbor notices how long they have gone missing, something which usually happens only when the old person with one or two broken legs is already decomposing or at least far too dehydrated to be saved, he the patient would be fine, he was lucky, he had been lucky in avoiding a severe trauma to the spine or the cranium, he was alive and conscious, he had not vomited and would not vomit until after the surgery when he'd vomit upon waking up from anaesthesia, nonetheless, in all honesty he had vomited a little bit before the surgery, that time not from the anaesthesia, but from stress, from an acute trauma to his *feelings*, he received a second text message from her, the first he had received soon after the cat-scan, we need to get you operated on, a doctor had told him, he had then been transferred to a room, he looked for the nurse, she was nowhere to be seen, the nurse who had taken his phone, she finally showed up, gave back his phone, he read the message, are you kidding me?, she had written, then nothing more, he wrote he was not joking at all, later he would explain what had happened, she didn't reply, he wondered if he should tell her he had had an accident, probably he should tell her about the accident, after all he was in a hospital with two broken legs and he would be operated on, he might die there in the hospital and she would never know about it, or maybe she would but quite later, and the truth might be mixed with lies, so and so telling her he had died while driving drunk or intoxicated with drugs, she knew he didn't drink or do drugs, but she might still believe she didn't know him well enough, he might be doing drugs in spite of everything, and be a boozer, a drunk who had wrecked his car on the road while traveling to get more booze or to meet a woman, and they could tell her he had travelled on such and such day, that day not being the right day of the accident, hence convincing her that he had travelled, drunk or intoxicated with drugs, to meet another woman, indeed no one knew he used to meet her, they would probably tell her he was going to meet a woman in such and such place, and not in *her* city, though in fact he was driving towards her city to meet her, that fact she was indeed supposed to know, she should know the truth, but then she didn't, for he had had an accident and so far refrained from telling her the truth, i.e., that he had had an accident while driving to meet her in her city, in her so-called city, thus called for it was the city she lived in, and now, if he died, she would probably learn that he had died in a car accident driving while intoxicated and travelling to meet a woman, who wouldn't be her, for if it had been her, not only would people not have told her he had been drunk and died while driving to meet a woman on a different day than the day he had had the real accident, but he himself would have told her he had had an accident when he was driving to meet her in her city, for no rational person would lie in these circumstances, in fact most people would eventually use this accident *to their favor*, for he had broken two legs and smashed his car against a guardrail to meet her, it might melt her heart, awaken in her a feeling of guilt which would render itself in tender care and ultimately develop into a sort of love, most rational people would aim for all the pity and compassion and kindness she would show after finding out he had broken bones and destroyed a car to meet her, despite this kind of accident occurring by chance, people feel guilty for being the indirect cause of those accidents, still he hadn't told her, he knew she was busy with a lot of work to do, she was skipping work hours to meet him, he didn't want her to waste any more time on him, visiting him in the hospital, feeling sorry for him, she should take care of herself, but then he knew her well enough to know it wouldn't work like that with her if he ever told her the truth, she would indeed feel pity for him, and guilty, so much guilt she would even reflect, possibly once he was recovered, she would reflect and conclude that she was bad for him, she made him waste precious time, time he needed to work and for himself, all those trips and long distance conversations, the face to face conversations, lunches, dinners, minutes waiting for her, he needed that time, she had told him so several times before, and it would be a thousand times worse if she found out he had had an accident when driving to meet her, so once he recovered from his injuries she would tell him they had to keep away from each other, he the patient couldn't be sure she would say that, but he believed she would act in this way, he had a true belief regarding her attitude towards their relationship in the aftermath of his accident, she would most surely wait for him to get better, to regain his health with no possibility of a relapse, she would say to him they shouldn't meet anymore, it would be for the best, each one of them should look for another person, and she was strong-willed, she wouldn't take back her decision, therefore he was afraid of telling her he had had an accident while driving to meet her, he didn't want to tell her he had crashed his car while driving to her city, his idea was to avoid any burdens on her conscience regarding his accident, he did not tell her what had happened when he checked his phone after being scanned, he read her reply and didn't tell her the truth, then the next day, before he went into surgery, she messaged and told him she didn't want to see him anymore, he consequently retched and vomited a little bit, covered his saliva-vomit stain under the bedsheet, didn't call a nurse, and afterwards he went and was operated on and when he woke up from anaesthesia he vomited for hours on end, she hadn't messaged him since the last time he had checked his phone, he hadn't tried to explain himself after the surgery either, both because he was ashamed and because he was vomiting and couldn't think clearly, he was confused, he hadn't replied and still had no news from her, now he had that friend of his, who wasn't even a good friend of his, visiting him, sitting on that chair, probably an uncomfortable chair by the way, hence he had indeed made the wrong decision, he admitted to himself he had made the wrong decision while trying to make the right decision, truth be told that was the usual story, *all people tend to make wrong decisions while trying to make right decisions*, it was possible although not probable for someone to consciously make a wrong decision, some people might do it and had probably done it throughout history, but usually people tried to make a right decision, even though they often ended up making a wrong decision, in some instances wrong decisions were fatal, like in extreme situations, in war a wrong decision could lead to a maimed limb or death, either of the one making the decision, or of someone else, he the patient thought to himself while watching TV.

Truth be told, driving too was a dangerous activity. How had he crashed his car against the guardrail? He must have made a wrong decision, or perhaps he had been the victim of a mechanical problem, though in that case he could still have made the bad decision of using a car with a mechanical problem or of not taking the car to a repair garage for inspection. Everything was a decision to be made, to be alive was to make a decision, and quite often the *wrong decision*, to decide to be alive was arguably oftener more of a wrong than a right decision, he thought while he watched an entertainment program on the TV, whose host was screaming like a goat. His ears hurt and he looked once again for the remote control, and he soon remembered his friend had it with him. To remain alive was indeed quite oftener than not the wrong decision, still, so far, he had opted to remain alive, despite all the obstacles and disgraceful events blocking his path. To remain alive was usually the worst decision possible, anyone should recognize that, yet people didn't use their brains, that being one of the main reasons for remaining alive to be the wrong decision, the fact that people in general were stupid was an obnoxious inescapable truth, and this included people who first seemed to be intelligent or at least had the potential for being intelligent, so most people were stupid and then many of the ones who weren't intrinsically stupid ended up by being stupid anyway, or at least stupid in certain situations or areas or fields of knowledge. People didn't use their brains, more and more people would say they wanted to give their minds a break by listening to disgusting mainstream pop or rap music or by reading awful moronic mainstream literature or by watching revoltingly embarrassing films and series; this worrying reality applied to all mankind, to every nationality, and this is an important assertion for all dialectical relationships he may want to establish, since he used to focus his wrath and disgust on his own nationality, as was only natural, for one tends to focus on and to discern and to notice details of things closer to them, his country and their inhabitants among these close-to-heart-and-eyes facts, but afterwards he had—sadly—concluded that *all mankind was generally stupid with a few exceptions*, and maybe some nationalities and societies were a bit more developed in certain aspects of life, thus allowing their citizens a higher degree of freedom and well-being, but the truth was that they too were societies where most people were dim-witted, so they all wanted to give their minds a break, even though he couldn't, for the sake of his life, tell when and how they had tired their minds, for apparently they had never used them, their minds and brains were still fresh, and if they had used neither their minds nor their brains, they had not wearied them, in short, they would never have to give their minds a break, for resting follows tiring, and on this he had already reflected several times. He got angry whenever he heard someone say they needed to give their minds a break with a light song, film, book, he immediately despised that person and would never respect them again, he pondered once again when his friend the visitor grabbed the remote control, which he had on his lap, and he the patient and gazer and thinker thought a bit more.

She won't ever forgive me where's that phone goddamn it, he the patient asked himself, groping around his bed in search of his phone, and his friend the visitor thought he was looking for the remote control. Here it is, do you want it?, he asked. He the patient said no thanks, but didn't tell him what he was looking for, then he found his phone, checked it, no new messages from her, one or two messages from his phone company and a pizza delivery service, how did these motherfuckers get my number?, he thought to himself, and he vented his frustration by groaning. His friend the visitor misinterpreted his signals once again, which was most embarrassing, for besides not knowing if his friend the patient liked beer or even drank beer, he couldn't even interpret his signals, as now he thought he the patient was groaning from pain, indeed he interpreted his friend's groan as a sign of pain and not of frustration, but his friend was actually groaning out of despair, he felt some itching and even pain in his legs, for sure, but he was groaning out of despair for, first, not finding his phone, and later for not having received any new message from her, so he the patient felt his frustration growing into irritation when his friend the visitor asked him if he should call the nurse to get him some painkillers, not because he the patient didn't feel any pain, but mostly because he only wanted to get a message from her the woman for whom he crashed his car while driving to meet and not be bothered by that friend of his, whom he actually didn't know that well, and he once more felt how distressful it was to live among people, despite all his previous efforts to come to terms with people and society, he still found *mankind and people more loathsome and evil than helpful and necessary,* for people were stupid and would remain stupid, he himself included.

I'm really stupid how can I be here if I'm smart I can't be smart if I'm dealing with this idiot and lying here, just look at his stupid face, he thought to himself, he the patient rarely found intelligent people, people around him as people everywhere were generally stupid, he wasn't even looking for intelligent people or a genius like her, she was a genius, she's the smartest person I know the most intelligent affectionate human being ever to live on this earth she's the only real human I know also the only being who's more than human a perfect being beyond the restrictions and abilities of a normal human, he somehow concluded, being there are not many human beings not at all not many normal human beings and *not even many human beings* whether or not normal she's the best, he used to think and would think at least several times a day, he could extend his list of praises to nauseating levels for any reader, in fact any person reading this account, or his thoughts, or this account of his thoughts, can or could be easily nauseated, anyway he preferred to shorten it for one day he might have to write a text, any kind of text, or to talk about her, then someone who read his text may find it much too long, a text filled with praises or rather composed only of praising words, and he may need to talk about her to someone, and that person might find his praises too obnoxious, *his readers or listeners, friends as they may be, would probably find his descriptions of her too cringe-worthy*, but that was reality, both *his* reality and the objective reality, an objective reality considered as the reality accessible by most if not all humans, not necessarily human beings, but by humans, a reality exterior and thus apprehensible by this majority of humans' central nervous systems, a reality as apprehended by the organs of sense and central nervous systems of humans. Other animals with their different organs of sense and central or peripherical nervous systems were not included, he couldn't vouch for those animals, however, for humans with human organs of sense and human nervous central systems she was the most intelligent human being that had ever existed and existed at the moment on earth [his praise is, in fact, nauseating, as one can now confirm], from this perfect being he was separated by distance and misunderstandings lack of communication mistakes wrong decisions made in the past even in the last days, so the patient was frustrated and looked askance at his friend the visitor. The visitor had the remote control in his hand.

Who's this guy after all can't remember his name thought I could but I can't is he some friend of that asshole from the university what's that guy's name too gosh I can't remember I'm getting senile maybe it was the accident, he the patient thought, and then he remembered how a doctor had tried to inquire of him regarding the car accident, with the purpose of finding out if the patient's memory had been affected by the car crash, what do you last remember before hitting the guardrail, because he the patient had briefly lost consciousness and as far as he remembered he had overtaken a car that was moving too slowly, an old man with a cap on his head almost covering his eyes was moving like a snail on the motorway, he had overtaken the car and then lost control of his car, it was raining at the time, the cloudy sky had abruptly given way to a more than expected heavy rain, he had lost control because the old man was *both driving slowly and zigzagging* on the road, thus often driving in the

middle of the road, partly in the right lane, partly in
the left lane, therefore he the patient had to
manoeuvre his car to avoid hitting the old man's car,
he avoided it but his brusque movements led him to
lose control due to the sudden heavy rain flooding
the asphalt, he had sworn while losing his grip, he
was swearing still upon hitting the guardrail,
fucking croon these idiots fill the roads, he had
thought afterwards, these people must have
cognitive problems they're assholes by the way
complete assholes they drive like maniacs in the
cities and towns and villages and slowly on
motorways they're ridiculous they drive like
assassins they should be in jail and never again drive
a car they drive at eighty kilometres per hour near
schools and kindergartens and then at fifty or less
on motorways they're assassins maniacs perverts
destroyers of life, the patient had thought several
times before and once again now, so he had been led
to an accident and consequent injuries and loss of
property by a combination of dangerous driving by
one of his fellow human citizens and heavy rain. He
had indeed expected to find rain while driving
towards her city, heavy or light rain, but he had

never feared rain, not as a driver and not even as a pedestrian, contrary to what he felt regarding hail, he did not fear rain, he knew it encompassed some risks for those who drove, but he still didn't fear rain, now he had his legs in casts and he couldn't find a valid solution for his problems, he had to send her a message or call her, tell her he was in the hospital, tell her the truth, nevertheless, she could still be angry with him, not for him having had an accident while driving to meet another woman, instead because he had lied to her for three days in a row. Perhaps she wouldn't be mad at him for having driven and crashed his car while trying to meet another woman, but she could still be disappointed with him for lying to her, though it could be seen as a rational lie, but then it wasn't rational at all, *why hadn't he told her the truth from the start?*, she would wonder, and probably conclude that he was now lying to cover up some other lie or unpleasant truth, in short, she might be mad at him whether he told her the truth or a lie, for he could never get rid of his past, he could break all his bones and still he would never get rid of his past and his wrong decisions, and that friend of his was watching TV like he was at home, he seemed pleased with that disgusting TV program, the hosts were screaming again and waiting for the viewers at home to call their program, call us and pay us, they smiled at the cameras, come on, call us and spend your sweet money with this utter aberration, spend your hard-earned money, money earned working as bricklayers drivers plumbers doctors engineers firefighters cooks, send us your sweet money, all these people have learned nothing or next to nothing all their lives, they went to school and worked and lived in society and never ever learned anything besides stupidity and abject ideas and habits in order to follow the norm and be slaves of stupidity and dim-wittedness, he thought, it was revolting, as a kid he had hoped to find intelligent people at school and later at university, but in fact he had found the most abhorrent people at school and university, for he could only find, both at school and at university, the same people he would find anywhere around him and ultimately almost all the people there were in this world, with a few exceptions, most notably her, the genius with a fragile collarbone, she had once broken her collarbone, she had endured her injury with stoicism, she's tough no one can say she's not tough sweet and tough how can someone be so sweet and tough [nauseating again!] at the same time, he thought to himself, for it seemed these were two traits that didn't intersect, yet they did, she's marvellous, he thought, once again to himself, for he didn't want to tell someone about it, no one wanted to know about her, people envy other people's geniality and overall good qualities, so he kept quiet to avoid other people's envy and hatred, in this case his friend the visitor's envy and hatred, whom he didn't know that well, he didn't want to arouse his curiosity, he didn't want to talk, the day before he had a roommate for some hours, for a few hours in the afternoon the bed to his left had been occupied by another patient, a lady in her seventies, she arrived and told him she was in her seventies, young man, can you please tell me what time it is, please, she had asked him, and then she had told him her name and that she was in her seventies. Though he had asked nothing at all, the new patient had told him her name and that she was in her seventies, though she had not told him exactly how old she was, she could be seventy, seventy-one, seventy-two years old, and so forth, she could even be seventy-nine years old, but her exact age she had indeed not told him, and he hadn't asked either. She was staying in another hospital wing, she wasn't even supposed to be in that infirmary, she had had one of her ears operated on, she had a hearing problem, thus she usually spoke too loudly, because she couldn't hear clearly what she herself was saying, she had apologized for any inconvenience, he had nodded, I hope I'm not disturbing you, young man, she yelled at him, particles of her saliva spraying all over her bed, I won't be staying here much longer, young man, she had yelled, and once again she had sprayed her bed and the floor with saliva, he was lying in his bed, he had pulled the sheet over his chest, don't you worry, madam, he had replied, the room door was ajar, he could see the hospital staff walking in the corridor, the corridor was illuminated by yellow lights, his room by a bluish natural light coming in through the window, nurses and doctors were passing by, his neighbor the lady with a hearing problem and a padded ear told him a few facts about her and her family, she had been thinking of her long deceased uncle, an uncle who had died in

Argentina decades ago, she was still young when that uncle of hers had died in Argentina, because he was a blackleg, he only wanted to work, he was a working man, she told him, there was a strike in the harbour, and he was a hard-working man, he went to Argentina to work and earn money for his family, she his roommate in that hospital told him, he worked on ships, almost all my family used to work on ships, she told him, not anymore, now I don't have any relatives working on ships, she confessed to him the patient lying next to her, to her right, and she yelled that story of her uncle, lately she had been thinking a lot about him, she didn't know exactly why, but she guessed she was melancholy there in the hospital, all alone by herself, her family was far away, her children and grandchildren were living hundreds of kilometres away, several even abroad, she wouldn't get any visits for the next two days, now she was afraid *she would get out of the hospital before her children or at least one of her children got there to the hospital*, in fact the doctors had been extremely nice in letting her stay in the hospital, with that kind of ear surgery the patient could go home some hours later, the patient would usually recover at home, but they had let her stay, because she had some heart problems too, they told her she should stay for observation, but they had actually decided to let her stay a couple of days in the hospital because she had no relatives who could come and take her home that same day, anyway she wouldn't stay much longer in that room, excuse me, young man, she told him, I was thinking about my uncle, the one who died in Argentina, you see, there was a strike in the harbour, and the lady told him once again about her uncle who had been stabbed to death in Argentina, and he wondered in which Argentinian harbour he had been stabbed to death, but yet he didn't ask her about it, he remained silent, his legs covered by the bedsheet, he pondered calling a nurse to get some help urinating. He didn't call any nurses, the lady next to him kept yelling her stories, it was impressive how she could yell so much without ever tiring herself, she must have evolved all this time, he thought to himself, he the patient concluded that the lady lying on the bed next to his must have adapted her larynx to compensate for her deficient-hearing apparatus, so *she could probably yell for hours on end*, then she asked him to turn on the TV, and at that time he indeed had the remote control with him, he turned the TV on, she kept talking, have you ever thought about working abroad, young man?, you must be careful, she said, out there they kill people for working, and he nodded, he had never thought about it, working abroad, no, never, maybe flying a helicopter in Greenland, that would be nice, he heard they paid a lot of money to helicopter pilots transporting miners across Greenland, he should get a pilot license to fly a chopper over that ice cappy Greenland, perhaps he wouldn't have broken his legs, he surely would take less risks regarding car accidents on motorways, as in Greenland there existed hardly any roads, even less motorways, he would bet there was not a single motorway in Greenland, in Greenland he wouldn't break both his legs while driving on a motorway, he was pretty sure he wouldn't break both or even only one of his legs driving on a motorway in Greenland, yes, he should be a pilot, but then she wasn't in Greenland, he doubted she would ever be in Greenland, she might one day visit Greenland, but she would never live in Greenland, Greenland had nothing to offer to a person like her, and in fact Greenland had nothing to offer most people, the majority of people won't ever find Greenland appealing, at least before half the world is scorched and dead dry, by then in Greenland one could even possibly grow some carrots and cabbages, perhaps even trees and lentils, nevertheless right now Greenland had nothing to offer her.

Please be careful if you go abroad, young man, the lady next to him had yelled, don't worry, madam, he had replied, I'm not afraid of working abroad, he had then added, oh, my uncle wasn't afraid of working either, he wasn't afraid of anything at all, but he died, she had told him, can you please turn up the volume?, she had asked afterwards, and he had turned up the volume, the TV remained on and the volume loud until a nurse had come back to fetch the lady, she had said goodbye, he the patient with the broken legs had turned off the TV. Why don't I tell her I'm going to work abroad and that's why I couldn't meet her, yes, that's it, he had thought to himself, but presently he dismissed such a stupid idea, it made no sense, she would find out he wasn't abroad, and even if she didn't, it would make no sense, it would be better to tell her the truth, but then again maybe it was too late, he should have told her the truth from the beginning, he should have messaged or called her once he had arrived at the hospital, or even before, while he was in the ambulance, he should have asked for some help from one of the paramedics, now it's too late, he would both make an arse of himself and arouse her suspicions, she wouldn't believe him if he told her the truth only then, as he had concluded the day before, when the lady with a hearing problem was being dragged out of his room in a wheelchair, what an idiotic idea, he had concluded, and later he had not thought about the possibility of telling her he was abroad for work, for work or at least to be interviewed for a job, it would make no sense at all, for he was supposed to meet her the day he had the accident, if he told her he was abroad for a job interview, she would be mad at him, even madder than if he told her he had had a car accident while driving towards her city to meet her, for she would assume he had disrespected her, which would be far worse than telling her the truth, though in this case, i.e., telling her the truth, she would probably begin to get mad at him, but less so, and then try to get rid of him once he was well enough, yes yes yes he had thought all that over and over again it made no sense sometimes it made no sense often it did make sense, he knew her he believed he knew her she would sacrifice herself for his well-being if she believed he would be better without her she would avoid him he wasn't prepared for that, therefore he was avoiding her now, so, no new messages, he looked at the TV, his friend was sitting next to the bed, he was looking attentively at the screen, he the patient observed his friend, goddamn the guy is drooling he's truly drooling but what am I doing here yes the legs I should call her and explain everything maybe she'll forgive me for lying I had the best intentions it's awful when we make the wrong decisions and have to bear the consequences throughout our lives I've always made the wrong decisions then now what decision should I make look at this asshole it's amazing how it rains less and less how rain is rarer by the year by the month yet I had to have this accident while it was raining oh god why why do I have to suffer so much life is pain maybe I should end my life terminate my misery but not yet not yet I have to call her what shall I say to her that last message I don't know she's angry of course I'm stupid completely stupid how could I tell everyone else and not her I told my mom sister my boss my friends even this idiot got to know about my accident it's awful only she doesn't know anything, he thought to himself, his friend the visitor was apparently watching the same program as before, now the hosts were pointing to a picture of a kitten and laughing, his friend was still drooling looking at the kitten, yes that's it I have an idea that's it, he thought to himself. He grabbed his phone and wrote her a message.

Sorry. I hope you can forgive me. I didn't tell you the truth. I have been in an accident and have spent the last three days in the hospital. A poor cat crossed the road and then I, he began to write.

Acknowledgments

I would like to thank Josh, Joseph, and all those who somehow work at or contribute to Long Day Press. Without you and your passion for (small) books, this book wouldn't be possible. Also, a big thank you to all my readers, especially my English-speaking readers, and in particular to those living in or hailing from the USA, who have so far been quite welcoming to this Portuguese author.

João Reis born in 1985, is a Portuguese writer and literary translator. His books are published in Portugal, the USA, Brazil, Serbia, and Georgia. *The Translator's Bride* was his first work to be translated into English, and his novel *Bedraggling Grandma with Russian Snow* was shortlisted for the Fernando Namora Literary Prize and was longlisted for the 2022 Dublin Literary Award. He's also the author of *A Devastação do Silêncio* (longlisted for Prémio Oceanos 2019), *Quando Servi Gil Vicente* (shortlisted for Prémio Fernando Namora 2020), *Se com Pétalas ou Ossos* (2021), and *Cadernos da Água* (2022).